A Monkey Grows Up

By Rita Golden Gelman
Illustrated by Gioia Fiammenghi

Scholastic Inc.

New York   Toronto   London   Auckland   Sydney

ISBN 0-590-41510-7

Text copyright © 1991 by Rita Golden Gelman.
Illustrations copyright © 1991 by Gioia Fiammenghi.
All rights reserved. Published by Scholastic Inc.,
730 Broadway, New York, NY 10003.

12 11 10 9 8 7 6 5 4 3 2 1   1 2 3 4 5 6/9

Printed in the U.S.A.   08

First Scholastic printing, March 1991

Vervet monkeys live in Africa.
They grow to be about 18 inches tall.
They usually weigh between four and eight pounds.
Vervets have light brown hair on their backs,
white hair on their bellies,
and bushy white brows and cheeks.
They are adults when they are four years old.

Vervets live in troops of 10 to 50 monkeys.
Most of the monkeys in a troop are female.
Males leave their birth troop
when they are between four and five years old.
Females spend their whole lives in the same troop.

This is the story of one little vervet monkey.

It was dawn.

Elephants were drinking at the water hole.

A herd of impala was leaping toward the rising sun.

Two giraffes were eating the leaves of a fever tree.

The monkeys were stretching, staring into space,
slowly starting the day.
One monkey was squatting next to a berry bush.
She was giving birth to her baby.

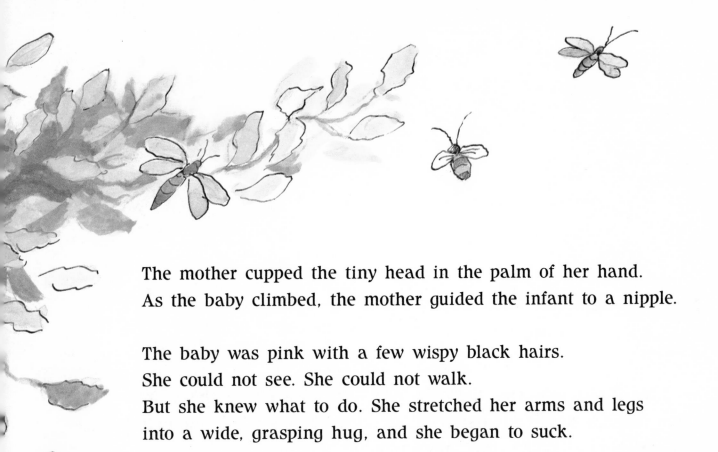

The mother cupped the tiny head in the palm of her hand.
As the baby climbed, the mother guided the infant to a nipple.

The baby was pink with a few wispy black hairs.
She could not see. She could not walk.
But she knew what to do. She stretched her arms and legs
into a wide, grasping hug, and she began to suck.

For the first few weeks, the baby was always at her mother's breast. Her mother's milk tasted sweet, like the blossoms of the umbrella tree. All day and all night, the baby snuggled and sucked.

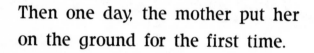

Then one day, the mother put her
on the ground for the first time.

The baby squealed.

A young female scooped up the baby.
She ran around in a circle.

She ran in and out of the bushes.
Then she gave the baby back to the mother.

13

As the weeks went by,
the baby spent more and more time
with young female baby-sitters
and with other baby monkeys.

She learned to eat the sweet flowers
of the umbrella trees.
The taste reminded her of her mother.
She ate the red and white berries from the bushes.
She learned how to take the beans
out of the fever tree pods.

But she still needed her mother for milk.

When the rains came, the little monkey huddled
with her mother in a tree.

And when it stopped raining, she splashed in the mud.
She nibbled on the new grass.

And she played with the other little monkeys.

She still went back to her mother for milk,
but not as often as before.

When the little monkey was three and a half months old,
she finally looked like a monkey,
and her mother knew that the baby
did not need milk anymore.
Now, the little monkey could not get milk
whenever she wanted it.
Sometimes her mother pushed her away.

The first few times, the little monkey was angry.
She threw temper tantrums.

But soon she learned that it was fun
to be on her own.

She loved to follow her older brother around.
They chased each other from tree to tree.
They jumped into the bushes.
They wrestled with the other monkeys.
Sometimes they even nipped at each other.

The mother watched from a distance.
She knew the young monkeys
were not fighting,
because when monkeys play,
they make a play face.

21

The little monkey learned how to catch grasshoppers
and how to find juicy larvae underneath leaves and stones.

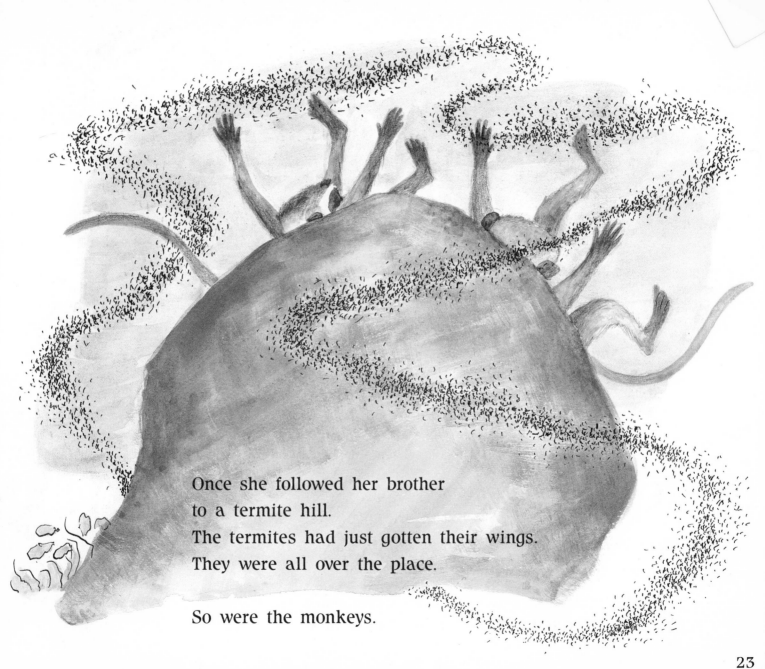

Once she followed her brother
to a termite hill.
The termites had just gotten their wings.
They were all over the place.

So were the monkeys.

23

One day the little monkey was grooming her mother.
Grooming is when one monkey combs the hair
of another monkey with its fingers, looking
for ticks or fleas.
The little monkey had just pulled out a flea

and popped it into her mouth
when some of the other vervets began screaming.
They were making strange, scary sounds
that the little monkey had never heard before.

All the monkeys stopped what they were doing
and ran to the highest branches of the trees.
The little monkey did, too.
After that she knew what to do
when she heard a leopard warning.

She also learned to recognize an eagle warning.
When eagles were nearby,
the monkeys ran into the bushes.
Leopards and eagles like to eat vervet monkeys.
Monkeys who belong to the same troop warn each other
when an enemy approaches.

27

A monkey troop is made up mostly of mothers and their children.
Monkeys who live in the same troop share their land, their trees,
and their food.

Some families in a vervet troop are more important than others.
When the little monkey was one year old, she discovered
that she was from an important family.

28

Early one morning, she saw an older female monkey
eating red berries.
She walked over to get some.
The older monkey looked up.
She knew that the little monkey was from
a high-ranking family.
The older monkey made a grumbling noise.
Then she walked away, leaving the berries
for the young monkey.

Monkey troops are not friends with their neighbors.
One day the little monkey saw a group of strangers
come across the border.
Four female monkeys marched over to the strangers
and stared at them hard, without blinking.
The strangers stared back.

Then more monkeys arrived and started to stare.
Soon there were two lines
of monkeys bobbing up and down.
They made angry sounds.
They shook their heads.
The lunged at each other, but they never touched.
After three minutes, the strangers left.

A few months later, during the dry season,
the little monkey felt a hot wind.
She saw a swirling wall of dust coming toward her tree.

Soon she was coughing and covering her eyes.

She never saw the elephant who was looking
for some leaves to eat.

As the monkey was choking in the dust,
the elephant wrapped his trunk
around a branch and pulled.
The little monkey crashed to the ground.
She screamed.
The elephant was startled.
He began to stomp his feet.

Luckily her brother was nearby.

One morning, the little monkey discovered
that her brother was gone.
He was four years old.
Like all grown-up male monkeys,
he had to find a new troop,
where he could have his children and live out his life.
The little monkey would probably never see him again.

All that day the little monkey moped.

But the next day, she heard a baby squeal.
Suddenly, though she had never done it before,
the little monkey ran to the baby and scooped him up.
She touched his pink head.

She touched his back.
She touched his arms.
She ran into the bushes.
She ran out again.

In two years the little monkey had learned about food,
    about friends,
      about enemies.

Now she was nearly grown-up.
It was time to learn about babies.